Little John Bear
in the
BIG CITY

by BERNICE MYERS

0196

Four Winds Press   New York

To Mary with love

Library of Congress Cataloging in Publication Data

Myers, Bernice.
    Little John Bear in the big city.

    SUMMARY: Little John Bear experiences some typical
big city experiences as he travels there to borrow a fur
coat from his friend.
    [1. City and town life—Fiction.   2. Bears—Fiction]
I. Title.
PZ7.M9817Li   [E]   78-15595
ISBN 0-590-07601-9

Published by Four Winds Press
A division of Scholastic Magazines, Inc., New York, N.Y.
Copyright © 1978 by Bernice Myers
All rights reserved
Printed in the United States of America
Library of Congress Catalog Card Number: 78-15595
1 2 3 4 5 83 82 81 80 79

"Your cousin Mark
is getting married today,"
said Mama Bear.
"And we're all going
to the wedding."

"I'm not going,"
said Little John Bear.

"No!
Just look at my coat.
It's all worn off
at the elbows."

Mama Bear
tried to hide the
worn spots.
But that only made things worse.

"Maybe I can borrow
my friend Herman's
fur coat,"
said Little John.

"Good idea,"
said Papa Bear.

Little John ran
for the bus.

But it was
so crowded
he couldn't get on.

So Little John
had to walk to
Herman's house.
Herman lived
in the city.

9

Little John
had never been
to the city before.

There were not many
trees
and hardly any berries
to eat.

THE YANKS WILL WIN.

EAT AT
ALVIN'S
DINER

And everyone
seemed to be
in a big hurry.

Still,
Little John
liked the city.
Wherever he looked
there was something
exciting
to see.

"A cave,"
said Little John.
"I wonder who lives in it?"

He didn't have to
wait long
to find out.

Coming toward him
was a huge monster.
The noise it made was
frightening.

13

When it stopped
to rest,
Little John
was pushed inside.

The monster stood
very still.

Then slowly
it began to crawl
through the tunnel.
Faster and faster
it went,
rocking wildly from
side to side.

It stopped once more
to rest.

Little John
jumped out and
ran up the stairs.

He was glad to be
in the street again.
He looked around.

"I wonder how far
Herman's house is
from here?"

A policeman
showed him where
to go.

"Just across the street
and down the block."

18

At the corner
some people were
standing and watching
a red light.
When it turned
green
they all ran
to the other side.

"It's a game,"
thought Little John.
He ran too.

But before he
could reach
the other side,
the light turned
red again.

Some people
were working
on a building.
Little John
stopped
to watch them.

ART
SHOW

VO

Suddenly
the beam he was
standing on
was
lifted
off the ground.

"Hey,"
shouted one of the
workers,
"get that nut down from there."

"Listen, wise guy,
if you want a job,
see someone
in the office."

But Little John
didn't want a job.
All he wanted
was Herman's fur coat.

At last Little John
reached Herman's house.
He rang the bell.

No one answered.

He rang again.

No one was home.

24

Disappointed,
Little John
was about to leave.

Just then
the door opened wide.
There was Herman,
dripping
wet.
"I was in the shower,"
he said.

Little John
hugged his friend.
He didn't mind
getting wet.

"Sure, you can borrow
my coat,"
said Herman.

"I'll bring it back
after the wedding,"
said Little John.

Little John
thanked Herman.
He promised to stay
longer
the next time he came.

Then he ran home.

"Let's hurry
or we'll be late,"
Papa Bear said.

"Don't worry,
we won't be late,"
Mama Bear said.

"Let me carry the present,"
said Little John.

The whole family
went off to the wedding.

And everyone had a wonderful time.